TALES FROM THE

ROOFTOP

Sandra Tena

With much love and brightest
blessings to Jo,

from Sandra xx

Clarity Found Editions

Printed by Book Printing UK
Remus House, Coltsfoot Drive, Peterborough, PE2 9BF

TALES FROM THE

ROOFTOP

Short, flash, and micro stories; thoughts, philosophical considerations

and subtleties;

and a poem in thirteen parts, joyful and ethereal, maybe just to bring

smiles…

For my family,

For my friends,

For my teachers.

Everyone, so far and so close,

I wouldn't change you for the world.

To everyone who has taken this little piece of my soul in their hands,

Thank you.

Contents

Pg

* *Pigeons*: Shortlisted story in the competition *Cada Loco con su Tema*, Mexico 2013, published in the anthology of the same name by Grupo Editorial BENMA

** *Visitor* and *Treasure*: Shortlisted stories in the competition *Voces sin Fronteras II*, Canada 2012, published in the anthology of the same name by Alondras Editions

Note on the 2017 translation: *Soddit the Cat* exists only in the English version, just as *DENUNCIARON A UNA MUJER QUE DEFRAUDÓ VENDIENDO PIES DE CASA* exists only in the Spanish version. Learn both languages and be lucky enough to have both. *winky face*

PART 1

THE VAST ENDING

Short, brief, and flash stories… light particles
from the deepest corners of my mind.

Dear reader:

These stories are all a product of my imagination, and as such, they are purely fictional. All of them, except *Let go* and, obviously, *Pigeons*…

…and I sometimes wonder if *Visitor* too…

Words mean more than we mean to express when we use them; so a whole book ought to mean a great deal more than the writer means.

- Lewis Carroll

What Red Had coming to her

'What the hell were you thinking, girl? Never mind how stupid it was you talking to a stranger along the way, and telling him exactly where you were going, and what for, but not even noticing the stranger was a wolf? A wolf! And then that woodman and the police blaming me and your father for not educating you right. Thank your lucky stars that good woodman was walking by at exactly that moment… and even more that he managed to get Granny out alive and kicking! That we didn't educate you rightly… blimey, girl, we've always bragged about what a model daughter you are… and now you come in with this sheer stupidity. Not recognizing a wolf… not just when you saw him along the way, but even worse, when you saw him in Granny's house! How could you not notice that it wasn't Granny? Granny does not look one bit like a wolf, let me tell you, so don't come and say that you didn't recognize her ears and eyes! And the muzzle! Granny has nothing whatsoever that looks like a muzzle! No, child, I can't even begin to understand what the hell was going on in your head. Go to your room. A month grounded and six weeks without baking anything. And don't talk back, you know well enough you had it coming!'

Pigeons

Any resemblance with reality is not purely coincidental.

'Croo, coo; crooo... croo; croo, coo,' flap-flap, 'croo,' a louder flapping of wings. 'Crooo, coo; croo, croo, croo,' and a whole series of wing-flapping sounds that made Federico sit up on the bed. But he lay down again immediately, covering his head.

A hundred and thirty pounds a night and he had a family of pigeons living in the air ducts.

'Coo, croo, coo.'

His meeting was at eight next morning, didn't the pigeons know that? He lifted the covers to look at the digital clock on the night table: 3:57.

Bloody pigeons.

'Crooo!'

Yes, you, blasted things.

Federico covered his face with his hands, groaning. Those pigeons hadn't let him sleep at all during the whole night. Annoyed, he called reception and – forty minutes later – they sent someone to solve the issue. Needless to say that by six he had already exercised, showered and got ready, with his case packed and a coupon for a free night next time he visited the hotel.

Next time. Bah! As if he would go back there. Sure, he'd be back to use the coupon, but after that time, never!

Any problem, Federico? asked his boss, who led the meeting. No, no, sir, carry on.

Oh, but he was so horribly tired.

After his continental breakfast, he'd left the hotel fuming, lethargically, and got into a cab. His boss had lodged at the hotel of the meeting, a five-star, while he had to do in the other one.

'Croo!'

Federico startled.

Federico, what on earth's the matter? Nothing, nothing, boss, I just thought I heard something strange, that's all. Fine, Federico, pay attention now.

Poor Federico, though, the more he tried to concentrate, the more pigeons he heard.

'Croo, coo; croo. Croo, croo; croo. Croo; croo.'

And wing-flapping.

For God's sake, where could those bloody pigeons be now? Could it be that the air ducts were not working here either? Cautiously, he raised his hand, trying to feel whether there was any air flow in the room or not.

Yes, Federico, do you have a question? Er, yes boss, what's your plan to raise the sales? Aren't you listening, Federico? We've already changed the adverts. Oh, um… yes, boss, but, I meant, er… internally. Well, Federico, that's a good question.

Phew, saved for now.

'Croo.'

So be it, he thought, at least I'll sleep on the plane.

Once at the airport, he and his boss went to get a cuppa while they waited for their flight.

What on earth's going on with you, Federico? Well, boss, the pigeons didn't let me sleep all night. There was a bloody family of pigeons devoted to keep me awake. And they succeeded. Then I heard them again during the meeting. You heard pigeons during the meeting, Federico? Blimey…

'Croo, croo.'

There they are, boss, you can't hear them? No, Federico, I don't hear them.

'Coo, croo.'

There's no way that they came all the way to the airport. They're not here, Federico, I think they left your mind a bit wobbly. No, boss, I do hear them.

As they got on the plane, Federico relaxed. There wouldn't be any pigeons here. He reclined his seat, closed his eyes and—

'Croo!'

No! Pigeons? How could there be pigeons on the plane? And the wing-flapping.

He got off the plane shaking. He'd been unable to sleep again. Because he only had his hand luggage with him, he rushed out of the airport, got in a cab and got home. He hurried into his room, took off his clothes and got into bed. No one and nothing would disturb him now. He put the covers up to his head.

'Croo...'

Shortlisted story in the competition Cada Loco con su Tema, *Mexico 2013, published in the anthology of the same name by Grupo Editorial BENMA.*

Better

And in that very moment, Elektra realised that younger men also have a charming side.

Understand-ments

The Prophet's Pyramid rose in front of her, imposing and enchanting. A chain floated inches above the first step, high, solid and sharp; yet there was no one around to keep the rules from being broken.

She climbed onto the first step and her mind grew clear, so she began the ascent. After the fifth step she realised just why it was forbidden to climb and she began the descent.

Visitor

As I was getting ready to leave that morning, I looked out the window and I saw him standing in the middle of the garden in front of my house. I recognized him at once, it was Athos.

It was good that it was Athos and not some pirate, or worse, an orc, like last week.

But such a shame it was Athos, because that morning I was in a hurry and I had to get to school.

Shortlisted story in the competition Voces sin Fronteras II, Canada 2012, published in the anthology of the same name by Alondras Editions.

Consequences, part I

After three hours and forty-seven minutes – which were worthless to count, because there wasn't anybody left who would count anyway – late as always, Epimetheus arrived.

The Woman who Only Wanted to Marry Orlando Bloom

It was in December 2001 when Alba Domínguez fell in love with Orlando Bloom.

She watched his movies constantly and read every magazine that mentioned him. Even knowing how difficult it would be to ever meet him, she made a very serious oath that she meant to never break: to marry only Orlando Bloom.

'You're crazy,' said her friends.

'But you're only twenty-one,' said her family, 'you'll meet so many men yet.'

'I don't care,' she said. 'I will only ever marry Orlando Bloom.'

By 2011, Alba Domínguez was still true to her promise. She was working as the editor in a newspaper in Durango, always hoping that the media would allow her to meet her platonic love. She got pregnant that year.

She had a beautiful daughter, and her boyfriend asked her to marry him. The best that Alba Domínguez could do was to move in with him.

Years later, Orlando Bloom got married. Alba Domínguez' heart plunged at the news, but still she would not break her promise. Coincidentially, she got pregnant again.

'Now let's get married,' said her boyfriend.

'I can't,' she said. 'Let's carry on as we are.'

It was then that a very important newspaper in Mexico City hired Alba Domínguez. Nobody was surprised when she broke off her relationship.

Settled in her new environment, she still hoped to interview Orlando Bloom, but it seems that their paths would never cross. He was still married; and although she was dating other men, it was never anything more.

She went to England once with her family, but she never caught sight of her actor.

Her children grew up. Her daughter finished university and married some time later. Her son got into an English university and she would visit him regularly. Life carried on.

Years passed and she was twice a grandmother. She retired and lived as a writer. When she was elderly, her children got her a place in a prestigious retirement home in London.

It was in 2049 when Orlando Bloom's wife died. Alba Domínguez didn't feel any type of joy. She felt sad about the pain that the actor might be experiencing.

One evening she was walking about the home's garden when she saw an old man she hadn't seen before.

'Are you new here?'

'Yes, I got here two nights ago.'

Then she recognized the man she was talking to.

'Could it be? Are you Orlando Bloom?'

The man smiled, humble and simple, as he normally did in interviews or press conferences.

It was in October 2052 that Alba Domínguez married Orlando Bloom.

The Tower of Babel

'Angel and I broke up.'

'Harsh. How are you feeling?'

'What time were we getting together to do the assignment for Marketing class?'

'How long were you two together?'

'At five. At Sylvia's.'

'How long for the World Cup, do you know?'

'Three weeks.'

'Two months.'

'You need to spend a little time on your own. Get a hobby, like a sport.'

'You say that because you're obsessed with sports. What you need is painting or writing, something that allows you to connect with your soul.'

'Sylvia, are we eating at yours?'

'Even if it wasn't that important?'

'What do you mean by important?'

'Well, the info about each country's team members has been announced, right?'

'Of some countries, maybe. Perhaps you can find that information on line... Why are you interested all of a sudden?'

'Because Jacob doesn't stop talking about it, so I want to understand a little bit more.'

'Nope, not even listening to you, we'll fix it later.'

'You're taking it very well.'

'You still need some time on your own, because you were still a long time in the relationship...'

'Because of the friendship, you mean?'

'Remember that trip we all did a while back?'

'Is that where you noticed?'

'Yes, sadly.'

'Well, it's always nice to travel, isn't it? With your partner, single, with friends, on your own.'

'They say that Chicharito is really good.'

'Are you just noticing?'

'What about the arts? Do they seem appealing to you? Searching for new ways of expression and all that.'

'I don't know… I'm too busy at work to pay attention to anything else.'

'That's harmful, too.'

'Don't tease me. The important thing is that I'm shifting a paradigm.'

'For a man? Are you sure that's what you want?'

'You've travelled a lot with your partners, haven't you?'

'Not so much… only a few times with Phillip, because all the other times it was always joining each other on work trips, theirs or mine. Maybe four of five times. Not really as a couple. But this last one to the Bahamas was a real holiday. Very romantic.'

'So are you coming over to watch the games with us, then?'

'Sometimes. Maybe.'

'You never felt bad about not going on a honeymoon?'

'No, because we knew we'd be able to take a special trip sooner or later.'

'Well, just between us, I'm the one who broke up with Jake.'

'I'm not that ill-informed. I was happy when I read he'd been signed by Manchester United. What an honour for him, and what a joy for us Mexicans!'

'That's no secret!'

'Angel was smothering me, I just couldn't take it anymore.'

'Of course, it's brilliant that he got signed in England. But my question is, is it for him or for yourself that you're making the change?'

'Speaking of which, is Phillip coming?'

'Yeah, he's just seeing a supplier.'

'So, everybody knew?'

'I don't know if everyone, but that's not the point. The important thing is that you realised it in time.'

'What I mean is, even though there are plenty of girls who are true followers, that doesn't mean you have to change to fit in... Not with him, not with us, not with anyone.'

'And what annoyed me most is that he always got things his own way, but when he didn't he would blame me that he never got what he wanted.'

'Look, look, look, they're showing pictures of Glastonbury on the telly. Looks lovely!'

'It's not that I don't like it, it's that I'm not attracted to it.'

'Exactly.'

'You can't wait to move there, can you?'

'What I hate is that I didn't notice earlier... I had so many years to.'

'Yes, it's time.'

'I'm tired of yelling here in the bar, aren't you? Shall we ask them if they want to go for a walk outside?'

'Don't waste your energy. It's not up to you to be changing people, no matter how close friends you are.'

'Nah, they're all so deep into their own conversations.'

'Wow, Carlos and Selena look so much alike... I don't know why it catches me by surprise even now.'

'The important thing is that you've noticed now, so you can do something about it starting today.'

'If he's asking you to change, he's not entirely worth it. No matter how good looking he is, or how much we all like him.'

'Yeah, side by side they look like copies of each other.'

'Yeah, let's tell them, so that we can get out into the fresh air for a bit.'

'Do you have a date for it, by the way?'

'I'm not so sure.'

'Of course we can.'

'We'll miss you.'

'I do have a bit of fun watching it, but only with friends.'

'I feel like it's not so big a change. In fact, I can change my mind if it's not what I thought it'd be.'

'In the beginning it was only because of the new job, but now that I've been there in person it makes me excited.'

'I feel so much surer of myself now.'

'We all know that you're worth it, and even when you're not hanging out with us doesn't mean you're not part of the group.'

'It's the thing about being independent, right? It's true, you've always been more independent than us, and that deserves a bit of recognition.'

'We're all looking for our place. Some move from place to place, and others move only internally, but in the end it's all the same. Movement is movement.'

'We're really going to miss you. You're a great person too.'

'I completely agree!'

Klimt's Nightmare

We went to see The Doors in concert. Because there weren't enough people, so not enough tickets were bought, we had to go without the magic of watching The Doors.

Disappointed, we went to get some tacos. My boss' friend, Joshua, noticed me; I noticed him, too. After dinner, we went to the bar where he worked, it was all friendly and laid-back. My boss and his wife decided to go, but Joshua, along with his brother, my friend Clara and I wanted to carry on partying.

So now, without the judicious stare of my boss, Joshua kissed me.

In the beginning it felt like it could work. He hugged me, he said that he wanted to know me better, that he liked me a lot, that I was one of what he called "the worthy ones". He asked me to the cinema and back to the bar for the next evening. It seemed like we were a perfect match.

But the night was not yet over for me. We all went over to Clara's house, and things took a turn. He started kissing me disproportionately. I say disproportionately because he seemed to want to make my entire face fit into his mouth. I couldn't understand it; I wasn't sure whether he wanted to kiss me or eat me. At a certain moment, I was sure that I could feel his upper jaw on my left cheekbone and his lower jaw under my chin. And teeth, teeth everywhere. Months later I saw a demon do exactly that in a movie.

I took Clara aside to decide what I should do. If I wanted, I could take him to the guest room. No, Clara, I just met him, how can you suggest that?

But he looks so interested.

Well, he might be, but he doesn't kiss too well.

Oh, darling, you can fix those things, it's only a matter of teaching him.

When I got back to Joshua, he had the sofa all ready for us. He wanted me to climb on top of him. I refused. He continued to kiss me anyway. His tongue in my mouth and on my cheeks and in my ears, and on my neck and on my nose and on my chin and on my forehead; he only missed my hair. And his teeth... I had never been so aware of another person's teeth. I had no idea how to avoid him.

The night was finally over. I'll see you tomorrow at 5 at the cinema.

Yeah, yeah, see you tomorrow, bye.

People often ask me why I still gave him a chance. Maybe because he was my boss' friend? Maybe because I was desperate for a man? Maybe because I haven't lost faith in humanity? Or maybe it was just that I was bored? Maybe we will never know the answer.

The next day at five o'clock everything changed. Joshua was being more than indifferent to me; he barely kissed me and we got into the movie, during which he didn't say one word. As soon as we came out of the movie, he left in a rush, saying that he had to be at the bar, but that he'd see me there that night.

I of course, had told my friends about the bar, and I'm so glad I did, because that night Joshua was even more indifferent to me than at the cinema.

After that, my phone never rang showing me his number.

*

Clara and I were waiting for our lunch in front of the Medical Sciences building at the university, when he walked up to us. I was taken by surprise at how openly he said hello to us.

I just stared at him.

What, you don't remember me? It's Joshua, Michael's friend. We met a few months ago, at the concert that The Doors didn't give because there weren't enough ticket sales. We even went to the movies later.

I was still just staring at him, not knowing what to say. The image of a whale shark crossed my mind, and a single phrase left my mouth: Well, no, sorry... I don't remember you.

He stared at me, flabbergasted. That's horrid of you, I hope you know?

Clara and I looked at each other as soon as he left, smiling knowingly. Oh, Clara, what if I told you that I haven't been able to get rid of the sensation of his mouth over these past four months: every time I bite into anything I get a weird feeling, almost like I'm embarrassed for him.

Just there

As the rain continued to fall, they decided to remain under the table.

Treasure

Sevilla walked along the aisles of the library. The book she was looking for was there, she knew it. Every clue had brought her to that place.

A delicate rain played her song over the glass panels. I have to find the book, finding it means my independence.

Something pulled her to the right. She had glimpsed a title in golden letters. Her heart leapt out of her chest.

She pulled the book out as if it were the most precious object in the world. She read the title once, twice.

She couldn't believe it.

She had it.

She held in her hands the Gospel of Light.

Shortlisted story in the competition Voces sin Fronteras II, Canada 2012, published in the anthology of the same name by Alondras Editions.

Consequences, part II

Watching him like that, from a distance, Pandora closed her box and left.

Soddit the Cat

His paws led him on many paths, wondrous and fantastic. Through hillsides and farmlands and a car park or two, and even a river at one point; he'd always known the Great Open Country would be like that, but he'd never imagined that three days into his journey he would already feel free, completely the owner of his own self... If there could only be someone to scratch his belly, then he would be in paradise! Granted, the weather was still quite cold, so he'd found himself daydreaming more than once of a blazing fire or a warm radiator in a lounge; the fuzzy blankets would be a cliché. And the cushion, too. And the plate of mouth-watering sardines or chicken left-overs... Or the bowl of milk – but then he remembered that milk made him gassy and that was why he had been sent away from his own home in the first place, so he pushed the bowl of milk aside in his mind and focused on the cushions and the hearty meals, and maybe a cosy lap. It was so good to have left Pilton and be free now, his own cat in his own land, yes sir!

He'd gone out looking for Wells. If the legends were true, Wells Cathedral was the one place he'd be able to find a good home, at long last, where the famous Louis, the Cathedral Cat, lived and would surely give him home if he knew his own sad story. If the rumours he'd heard were true, Louis was getting old and he already had a protégé in the Cathedral, young Pangur, who's been able to capture the attention of staff and visitors alike, so they'd maybe make room for another newcomer into the site. He'd hang out with them, learn their ways, see how they made it so easy for humans not only to accept them but also to treat them with great respect and adoration.

He could imagine both cats getting the attention of everyone around without having to give up an inch of their lounging space or an ounce of their dignity; from what he'd heard about them, they never performed any sort of cutesy attention tricks or needed to beg for food or cuddles: everything just came to them in the blink of an eye – and sometimes not even that! Every once in a while, the neighbour's daughter had said, people would just flock around one or the other bringing gifts and queuing up to stroke them and scratch behind their ears. Those were the tricks he'd wanted to learn.

He was getting tired of going so near the main road, though, even if it had just been a few hours. He knew that he was close to Wells because there were many cars now and a roundabout up ahead. The sign for Wells was a bit strange, though: it had more numbers than when he'd seen it first – it didn't make much sense, but he shrugged, at least as much as a cat can shrug, and kept walking. His heart leapt when he heard the sounds of the city: the voices, the laughter, the children at school and people greeting each other. He turned the corner and there it was a long street, sunny and comforting and full of potential laps, with a church tower all the way to the top. It was a lot smaller than he'd imagined it, but it might just be a situation of reality vs expectation. He raised his tail and walked up to it.

Only two or three people crossed his path. He could hear some say hello, but he kept his eyes on the church tower. The voices of the children were stronger to his left but none seemed to have noticed him. He didn't mind. A pretty lady with long black hair and chocolatey eyes knelt to stroke him as she cooed hello. As much as he'd liked being petted, he moved away as from his right a tall man with long brown hair leant over to kiss the lady.

'Cat's got priority today, I see,' he said.

The lady laughed, 'Well, he stole my heart for a moment; how could you not, little one?'

They tried to stroke him for a bit, but he slinked past them each time, then they got up and said goodbye and walked up the street, towards where cars were passing up and down at a faster speed. Her hair swung from side to side like a silk curtain, his ponytail bounced as they both laughed and kissed and laughed again. The lady seemed so crystalline, the man friendly and witty. He smiled as they walked away, then turned his attention back to the church tower. He'd been looking at it as he was being petted, and he'd finally decided that it was too small to be the cathedral – this whole street seemed too small to be a city, to be honest. Could be that it was probably just the outskirts, that he'd been overexcited about the tower and immediately made up a story in his head. He followed the couple as they turned into the street with more cars. He saw them walk up to his left in front of a tall building, old and fabulous with a picture of George and the Dragon hanging above the thick wooden doors, then walk into a green smaller door further away with the picture of a Green Man hanging above it. Other people walked around them, both men and women, most of them with long hair. Weird. He turned his attention to the right and saw a big church-like entrance, an impressive archway which spoke of radiant ornaments and warm radiators. He crossed the street and crossed the archway…

… and after wandering inside for a few moments, squirming away from curious humans and crossing a few glass doors along the way, he found himself back outside – in a big garden that expanded into eternity and high walls and pillars rising from the ground here and there, broken and majestic all at once. He meowed and ran towards the ruins of what had had to be a most impressive building indeed, sniffing around for food and warmth, neither one to be found among the wide field. It could not have been that the cathedral had been taken down all of a sudden, could it? It couldn't be that Louis and Pangur were purely legends?

He looked around a few times, meowing in confusion. A few humans tried to reach out to him, to comfort him and offer food at times, but he could not deal with them just then. Well, maybe with the food. He ate and purred obediently and moved away again as soon as he could, to try to find answers.

Then, all of a sudden, he saw a tower rising in the distance, on top of a hill that grew directly from folklore and fairy-tale… and he understood where he was. He had heard people talking about it with a touch of sarcasm back in his old owner's house. That was the Tor, these were the Abbey ruins, and he was in Glastonbury!

He sat down and washed his paws.

The next day, after a silent night between two rustic buildings and a lovely dinner that one of the waitresses from a café had brought out to him, he walked around the courtyard where he'd found his lodgings and sat for a little bit at the foot of a statue of a slim lady and a slimmer dog. They were both looking up at the sky, and he looked up as well. The sky didn't really show him anything, but he felt his spirits rise. He'd gone way off track, but he'd make do for a while, at least for regrouping and getting on his track again. He remembered seeing Glastonbury written a few times along the way, even outside the entrance to the Abbey, but since he'd never seen it written, it just hadn't clicked. How silly he felt, and embarrassed for his mistake. But so far people had been good to him, so it'd be fine. For a while. Just for a little while.

He came out of the courtyard and walked up the street, past the building with the picture of the Green Man, and past many shop windows that displayed dragons and crystals and faeries and brooms. A cat or two and owls and stags – and all those funny things that people liked to buy from movies and books that they liked. This was all too silly for him. A serious cat who wanted to be master of his own destiny did not belong in a town like this – a town with shiny lights and people in capes and shiny wings. They had nice velvety laps, though. And they smelled rich and homely, faintly like nuts. He saw a church to his left, small and pretty, and wondered if they had warm radiators inside, and if they would take in a cat.

As he crossed the gate he saw a set of lines to his right, and curious as he was, he decided to investigate. He put his nose to the first line and noticed that a great deal of human feet had traded on those lines, and soon he found out that they were actually paths. He followed one and realised that it folded onto itself over and over until he found himself in the middle of the circling lines. He sat there and observed the humans walking outside the church.

'Look, mummy, a cat did the labyrinth!' a childish voice said. She was pulling on her mum's hand to lead her towards the church gate, but the mother was in a bit of a hurry and said they'd be back later.

'Oh, look, so cute!' a couple of young women came to the gate and looked at him, as an older man stopped and chuckled before he carried on his way. 'Even Glastonbury cats are looking for the meaning of their lives,' he could hear him say as the women agreed and laughed.

'Look hun, I think it's the cat we saw yesterday,' a familiar voice said, clear and nourishing. He looked up, and sure enough there was the raven-haired lady with her hand to the iron fence, her man pressing close to her and putting his hand over hers. 'Brilliant!' he said, and kissed the top of her head. He was at least a head taller than she, and they looked happy and healthy and like they fitted in together perfectly. He wasn't entirely sure what that meant, but he liked that feeling the couple conveyed to him.

The morning passed and he went up the High Street, looking left and right at the colourful characters and the shiny and shimmery shop windows. A human or two greeted him, some only went "aww" and carried on, most seemed like they were walking inside their own little bubble. Everyone was dressed very differently, though, some in leathers or skins and long dreadlocks or plaits, some in flowing velvets and faces like they were dreamily sniffing a nearby skunk, some in glorious faery wings that called his attention every time they sparkled in the sun (but that he knew he must control his instinct to claw at, because for all the laughter their wearers shared, they might not be too happy at having a stranger come and shred them to pieces); old, young, middle-aged and children, most laughed or at least stared dreamily into space, many said hello to each other as they passed. Even those who wore the most normal clothes looked colourful and full of wondering, like they were trying to show life they were happy even though they were so confused. At some point he saw the child he'd seen from the church green as she said to her mum, 'See, I told you that when we came back he'd be out of the labyrinth!' The mother was still in a hurry.

Yet the feeling the town gave him was of warmth and joy, even in the cold season. He liked it. For a morning. He was a tourist and he'd make his way to Wells now, to find a proper home in the enlightened Cathedral, home of the cats. But as he reached the top of the High Street and saw the sign that said Wells, accompanied by a bunch of numbers, he felt a longing to look back to the street he'd just made his way on. It seemed like a town full of strange people, some hearty and comforting, like hot chocolate, some who probably hadn't showered for days, some smelling of flowers and spice, some like nuts and aubergine – still, most of them felt welcoming, and he wondered if he should stay. For a little while at least, until his need for experimenting was satisfied. He kept thinking of the couple he'd seen twice now, their merry laughter and loving tenderness.

Yes, he'd stay in this town for a little while. It wasn't as crazy as the reputation he'd heard about it… well, it probably was, but what harm could it do? He went back down the High Street, into the courtyard he'd slept the night before, and looked at the café door until the waitress saw him again and took out a nice meal for him.

He roamed around for most of the next day. The same kinds of people swarmed about, and he enjoyed himself immensely inventing their stories in his head. He'd peeked into a few of the churches but they didn't have the comforting feeling he'd hoped – he went back into the courtyard instead, unsure of whether he'd find a home there and be fed by the local cafes, or if maybe he could go all the way into the back and make himself a library cat (for the library at the rear courtyard seemed a friendly, if indeed frosty kind of place), or see what was in his cards.

He went and sat between the slim lady and her slimmer dog, and at that moment the tall man with the long hair came into the courtyard and started skimming the books that were in a stall against the wall. He shifted and the man noticed the movement. They caught each other's eye. For a moment he felt understood, and he thought he'd be happy to stay like that, frozen in time with his soul being read by someone else's soul – and the moment was broken by steps and the jingling of keys. They both turned to see the pretty black-haired lady, dressed in flowy skirts of bright colours, her back to them as she locked a green door almost in front of the stall. When she turned she broke into a smile and pressed her body to the tall man, both lost in a deep kiss and a trickle of happy laughter.

He thought the moment was gone, the other soul had ceased to pay attention to him and how he was alone again – yet he heard the man say, 'Before anything else, look over there!'

'Oh, our cat with the Wise Lady and her Pooch!' the lady crooned.

'Our cat?' said the man.

'Well, it's the same one! Unless Glastonbury was suddenly taken over by a swarm of black cats?'

'Swarm of black cats?'

'Herd? I don't know!'

They laughed again and held each other tight. They walked away and he could hear the lady asking if her man thought he belonged to someone nearby. He followed them.

He entered a loud, happy pub. The couple's smell had mingled with the others around them, and the music invited everyone to dance in their spot, so it took him a bit of time to find the man and lady again. Yet, when he finally spotted them, someone else caught his attention, and she was beautiful! She was curvy, not like the pretty lady was curvy, but more like round and sleek at the same time, furry as the warmest blanket, and her colours were an enticing combination of black and auburn and white. 'Calico-cat!' he heard the pretty raven-haired lady say as she bent down to stroke the tri-coloured fur, 'Hello, Millie!'

Ah, Millie, that was her name... he hid beneath a bench and watched as the couple danced and hugged and danced some more... they sometimes reached out to the cat and sometimes reached out for each other, and they looked just as happy as they'd done since the first time he saw them. But now there was Millie. He tried to clean himself, to look and feel more presentable, not like he'd been on his own for almost a week now. Just then he saw she'd noticed him. She stretched, coming out from a comfortable ball into a sleek fantastical creature. She bounced off her chair and came to say hello.

Both cats smelled each other, he elated and she trusting. What's your name? Millie asked him. I don't go with a name anymore; my family didn't like me, so I ran away after they shouted at me for something I didn't do – on purpose – and now I've become a wanderer and want to leave even that name behind, to keep no ties with those humans. How old are you? she asked him then. I was born in the summer, so I haven't been a year yet... almost there, though.

Well, Millie said, I've been here almost seven years and I can tell you for sure that you'll like it. You get so much attention and yet are a free cat, able to come and go as you will. Everyone will love you and if you play your cards right, someone or other will open the window for you at night. I would bet on that couple for you, they live just around the corner and would be happy if you joined them every now and then.

Seven years, he thought... she must think she's too old for me... I wonder if she'd be okay with it though... I wonder...

Just as he was considering whether she'd be a good enough reason to stay in Glastonbury after all, letting go of his wish to become a proper church cat, the friendly couple he'd been meeting spotted them both under the bench. 'Oh, look, Millie's got a friend,' the lady said as she knelt to reach out for him. Her lap seemed warm and welcoming, her ample bosom comfortable for curling up and having a good purr. He felt her hand along his spine and his whole body quivered with contentment.

Ah, sod it, he thought, and presented her with his belly.

Thysanura

I had chased him ruthlessly between the mats under the drum kit, and under the newspaper that was spread under the cats' litterbox, as if he was a *Navarro* and I was a King Juan II blinded by the thirst for vengeance.

But just like the clueless vengeful bloodhound, as soon as I spotted the silverfish at the corner of a mat, he would hide away somewhere else, and as soon as he popped up from under the newspaper and I lifted my foot to crush him, he'd rush away again. Maybe it was the flu, I'd think, feeling wretched at not being able to kill him and be able to get back into bed, as my eyes went all unfocused and I had to blow my nose again.

And that's how he had me going, lifting mats and newspaper and the litterbox, always hoping that the unholy insect – which has all my books and archives in a mess – wasn't more intelligent than it was seeming to me now, and get under the drum kit because that one I could not lift, not in this state, when he suddenly came out from under the newspaper.

I lifted my foot and let it down again with probably a lot more strength than was ever needed, ending thus the tiny existence of the sad little silverfish.

Consequences, part III

Because gods don't count time in the same way that humans do, during those ten days only an age had passed for the mortals: the life of a new hero, two wars, three demi-gods who'd come to solve the urban problem of men, and one more poem dedicated to Ragnarok.

Under the shadow of the pen

I find myself overwhelmed at the impossibility of writing another novel. *The Death of the Silver Fish* was a complete success: it took me to Europe, Japan, USA; it gave me the all banalities of fame, which I gladly took; it gave me prizes and accolades; it gave me entire nights of celebration and enjoyment. All seems perfect, doesn't it? It all seems like that dream that every writer wants to reach.

But now it's an entirely different matter.

Now my ideas have taken control of my mind, and they don't allow me to have any thoughts of my own, but instead they're there and talk and talk and talk and I can't even express my opinions. And even so I can't write, because it's impossible for me to follow the thread of all those ideas. I feel drowned in the huge quantity of characters that propagate and converge in my head, seemingly having no need to leave my head anymore. I already know some of them, from *The Silver Fish*, others fight over my attention and do everything they can to amaze me and make me write about them, and some of them are even of other's property, from Dumas' and Carroll's to Tolkien's, Ende's, García Márquez', and even Rowling's, and I know that's bordering on hallucination. What surprises me is that they seem to know me, and that I can have sensible conversations with them, if the word "sensible" can be used here.

Excuse me sir, I know you... You are Melquíades... But, what are you doing in my home?

Let go

You'll leave tomorrow and not return... Will I miss you? Yes, I will, I won't try to hide a truth that everyone knows. I'll cry for you, I'll pull my hair and cry for you, miss you forever and all the good things you gave me. But I've grown, matured, it's time to let you go and begin a new stage in my life. I have to be myself again, the real me, not hiding under the veil of you. And I will know for ever that once without you, better things will come.

Consequences, part IV

And they, poor souls, never saw what was left at the bottom of the box.

Für Bastian

I love you, Bastian, I never got to tell you, but I love you.

I love you and I don't think that feeling is going to go away.

I don't know what to do about it. I don't know if it's a good or a bad thing that I didn't say anything this weekend... What good would it do to know that you love me too if we can't be together anyway? Or what good would it do to know that you don't love me if that's only going to break my heart? The day we met seem so long ago, back there in my beloved Querétaro. When I saw you the first time I thought, "My God, I could really fall in love with that man". With your violin and your long, lean figure, with your golden curls that managed to cover your lapis lazuli eyes at the most untimely times. I was so right. And we talked, and we laughed, and we lived as if those were the happiest times of our lives. I wouldn't know if they were. You taught me all about poetry, music, Mozart, Beethoven, Benedetti and Baudelaire; about diving into the deepest parts of ourselves to bring out symphonies with our thoughts. I found meaning in the most meaningless things by your side. With you I learned what it is to feel as free as the wind of Querétaro. Believe me, I was happy with you, happy as I hadn't been in years, but I was also suffering sorely. Maddie was there, beautiful, amazing as always. And you were together, from the day I met you both. I adore her, it's impossible not to. Even now she stirs tenderness and admiration in me. Back then I couldn't stand hurting her. Now I know that things could've been different.

When I visited you I didn't suspect a thing. No one told me a single word. You still wore your wedding ring, as if it was a part of your finger. Even when you had written saying that it was all over two months ago, definitely. How many times did this one make now? Three? Four? Five attempts that clashed with the desire to be close to you above all others? Not from everyone, just from me, apparently. Was it only me?

You'd hide from my glance unnecessarily; from the recitals in Queretaro when you took advantage of your locks to avoid looking at me from the stage, to your half-written letters in which you wouldn't say any more than necessary. I should have accepted it, just like a farewell stretched by the instability of imprudent emotions.

How could I have been so blind, that even after flying across the ocean and entering your home you hid from me? How could I have been so blind that I never realised that Maddie's presence had become ethereal in your letters? How was I so blind that I couldn't see your pain when you saw me standing there?

And now you're so far away, and she's far away with you, forever in your mind, and maybe also in your heart, oblivious to the fact that she's said goodbye to us, to you and your restless love.

Strands of guilt move after me, along the German train lines, second by second, as I am now the one distancing herself. My life spins inside my head; the words I never said… the words I said… the words I yelled. The words you heard, the words I swallowed… the words that touched her ears even though it all seemed false.

You said it time and again, that it was really not my fault. What I said and what I didn't, that's something else. Another reality. Another lifetime, possibly.

Those were your words. Words, words and violins. You played again the day I arrived. You looked up at me from your place on the stage for the first time. Everyone met me and congratulated me; I don't quite know why, perhaps just because of social discomfort.

We walked around the squares and side streets of Cologne that night; you played another melody meant for me, sad and subtle, like the Autumn leaves falling into the water in a fountain or creek.

You told me your story, all the clarity of a reality that never existed. How she showed us one face when her real one was completely different; how in the end she stopped sighing and instead wrapped herself in screams and rants. How she had been like that from the beginning, how you already knew but didn't want to confront it; that you went back to her every time because of your family history, because you'd known her always, because you knew it couldn't be any different. That you saw her fall in love and couldn't do anything but offer her unconditional love; you had to stay with her because *he* couldn't stand her anymore. That all the while she kept going back to him over and over, after Querétaro, you couldn't do anything but tell yourself that she was happy and that this was the best thing for both of you. That when he decided that Maddie's moods would change only by staying with him permanently, that with a baby she was bound to stabilize, you stood back and watched her belly grow… that only then were you able to let her go. That when I told you the first time it had been your mistake not wanting to listen, not changing the last six years. That it wasn't my fault, you said over and over, and I add it here again because those words burn my skin.

You told me another thing, too: that I am who I've always been to you.

I couldn't ask anything else. You leave me with both a yes and a no.

It's probably just an illusion. The shield I carry. Never fall in love with someone from your own city, better to keep them as far away as possible. It's probably stupid of me; I don't notice things around me… and the fact that Maddie – either of them – did it too, or worse, is no comfort.

How could I really know what you feel for me? I would love to find a way that didn't involve a permanently broken heart. I would love to be sure of my own feelings. Keep her apart from you.

My heart aches for you. Forty-five minutes after we said farewell, my heart aches for you.

I think you love me too. I think you love me and that's why you shielded yourself in the party you threw so that all your friends could meet me… But if you also love me, well, than that's probably also an illusion.

Was that afternoon we spent laying under a tree, writing poems for the clouds, an illusion? Was that night when, after your concert, we walked over to Guerrero Square and you played your music between the fountains? Was it, really, an illusion when we passed in front of *Las Gardenias* right as the musicians played *Making Love Out Of Nothing At All,* and you took my hand to dance right between all the fascinated tourists?

You never cheated on Maddie; at least not with me. Or am I mistaken even in that fact, and those pleasurable moments constitute an infidelity already? And in that case, why? And why the ring still, after months from her goodbye? Is it then an illusion that we're the sensible ones and she's not?

I could ask myself those questions and even so never get an answer. I could waste myself in a new unfinished goodbye, or perhaps just close this chapter now and never look back. The problem is that this is something that we need to agree on. As long as one of us opens the door, the other one won't be able to keep from entering.

I wonder if it's good for us to keep these illusions alive, or should we risk the painful emptiness of reality?

Today the Rhine will continue flowing, and so will it do tomorrow, and for thousands, millions of years. And so will I, no matter what. The Rhine will continue flowing, and so will I.

The vast ending

I don't know how it happened, but one night, before the Sun came out, or maybe it was midday, I found myself walking along a series of ceaseless Borgesian forking paths. I have not been able to come out from there since. The walls that flank the paths are three times my height; I can't see to one side or another, just to the front and the back; the pink and violet skies above my head give away an ever-setting Sun. Night will never come, and I need to sleep.

I keep walking, conscious of each one of my steps, knowing that I don't want to turn back on them, knowing that I don't want to take the wrong turns again, conscious that the only way to find the exit is to keep walking.

I want to meet him. At times, even with my sight fixed on the path, I am thinking only about him. He told me to stay on these roads; that we will meet, someday… It's the most beautiful song I have ever heard. I was nineteen, and my boyfriend dedicated it to me. Absurd. Why would you, if you're dating someone, dedicate a song to them about two people who haven't met yet but are destined to? I didn't mention my doubts to my boyfriend, but instead I secretly walked and wished *he* would find me.

The path continues, and the corners follow one after another, and sometimes I reach a dead end and I have to walk back on my own steps, full of uncertainties and hesitation. Then I notice that that's the only way to get to the path that I should have chosen to begin with: beautiful, open and full of light, sometimes even with colourful flowers or amazing designs done on the stone walls.

When I'm walking down the wrong path, by contrast, I have to get spider webs off me, or walk over mud, and sometimes even end up in total darkness.

The search started, actually, when my boyfriend dedicated that song to me, I don't know how many years ago now. It all started because I don't know what human skin is. I don't know what a heartbeat is like. I don't comprehend substances, carbons or oxygen and hydrogen. All I know is that for years I was paralysed at the mere thought of contact, and that now I don't feel anything. Because an orgasm is a static moment in the air, and as it dissipates when I zip my trousers again, then I am left with nothingness after each encounter.

Sometimes the paths trifurcate, and then my doubt is absolute. Every time I make a choice I wish fervently and ask the gods for it to be the right one.

I am left with nothing after each encounter because every time I make contact my dream to study in London dissolves even more.

…Why is it that sometimes I lose the sounds and only the static remains, but not as an explosion of pleasure, but rather as secretions of a stigmatized reality?

During those moments when the world turns around me, when my sight goes dark and the hole in my stomach makes me falter, *ho paura*, there is no going back.

My feet drag on the stones, and I try to keep my eyes open in case he appears. I know he's waiting for me, and I need to get to London because that's where he is. I feel as if the walls have become tighter, I feel my heels screaming.

That's because I've not been with too many, but enough to mean something.

I realised this last night, or this morning, from which I haven't been able to wake up at all, while I came home at 4:27 carrying my high heels in my hands so as not to wake my parents up, going over my mistake of ending up parked out by the shooting range with a married man.

The static explosions weren't enough anymore, and the corridors get narrower and narrower, and the darkness lets in nothing but a single photon that I simply cannot reach.

I suppose I died.

I close my eyes and walk half-guessing, the roughness of the rock under my fingertips, my feet slipping here and there, humidity invading my lungs.

London gets farther and farther away. I feel new ground underneath my feet.

When light returns to my eyelids, I realise I've been reborn.

PART 2

THE LAUGHTER OF CATS

Thoughts, anecdotes and moments of deep awareness

Most cats, when they are out they want to be in, and vice versa, and often simultaneously.

- Louis J. Camuti

The perfect moment

Miles away from light at noon
Total eclipse of the moon
Many reasons to believe in life
Just listen to what it's telling you.
Enigma

The perfect moment does not exist. Don't misunderstand me, I'm not a fatalist or a pessimist; I'm not, to be completely honest, even a realist.

But there is no perfect moment, and when you look at the picture objectively and you realise the truth of this phrase, believe me that you can get a good chuckle from those moments which in their impertinent moment turned perfectly imperfect.

What a laugh, that first kiss, the very first of them all, that you were given under the Italian full moon, walking by a riverside, and that with a gruesome lick that startled you to the core, sent Moon, river and Italy itself to the rubbish bin.

What a laugh, that moment when you felt so free and sat in one of the many beautiful, peaceful squares of Querétaro and began to write what your sweet soul inspired you to, when the youth team of a famous political party arrived with their noisemakers, whistles and curses towards the other party, shaking all your inspiration to the ground.

What a laugh, when you, with your BA in International Relations and your extensive knowledge of Great Britain, told the president of the UK Education Association in Mexico that one of your favourite English authors is Oscar Wilde.

What a laugh, all those kisses that you weren't given, inspirations that never came out, and definitely, all those times you've made a fool of yourself – that can't be called otherwise – that made you lose sleep for days.

What a laugh.

Wait... I think I need to take back my words. Images, beautiful images from all kinds of moments are coming to my mind. What about that moment in the ranch, while you nap in a hammock as twilight falls, with not enough light to continue reading, and you listen to your family's voices, the ripples of laughter coming from the outdoor table where there is always food, and your sister asks about you, and your mum comes to look for you, caressing your hair, talking softly?

What about all those times of shared laughter, with those friends that you'll always keep in your memory, with your childhood friends, with those that you had in your life for one year, or with those that are around today?

What about that moment of full conscious realisation, as you looked through the telescope lens, that the bright object you were looking at was Antares, and you felt tiny, insignificant in comparison, yet so deeply satisfied?

What joy, such perfection.

Yet, curiously enough, you are not looking for perfection during those moments. Perhaps that's why those moments are perfect... The perfect moment is real.

Waiting room

Being original is coincidence, wishing to be so is a defect.
A. Chavilliers

If I had worn my red waistcoat today, the three of us waiting outside the psychologist's office would have looked exactly the same: jeans, boots, tight turtleneck and waistcoat. Fashion. But today I wore my sandshoes, my black leather coat, and my Harry Potter scarf, to go with my purple hair.

When I arrived, only one of the other ladies was there, with her three- or four-year-old son. There is no difference to me, I cannot tell the age of infants. She could have been my age. I imagined that he was the age my own child would have been. And again I thought it was a good thing I didn't have any children. The second lady arrived later, with her seven- or eight-year-old son. They knocked on the door of the children's therapist. She was still busy so they had to wait outside with us. Both kids sat down with the colouring book that one of them had brought along. The two ladies talked courteously between them.

There we were, the five of us, waiting for both psychologists to come out from their respective patients. I added two and two and I reached the conclusion that in that waiting room there were three grown ladies and three children.

Soliloquy

Remember that dream? Dancing in the school hallway... But, was it me or was it Azucena who danced? Was it me or was it Azucena who had the dream? Or was it...? After so many years without dancing, could it have been destiny? Was it telling me to wake up? Maybe it was a message so you could get back to yourself. A compelling calling from the soul.

Shadowlands

A misty and sleepy morning.

A tired morning.

A surreal afternoon, full of duskiness and of feverish dreams... full of spasms of pain that only dreams can cure... and a jerk of my feet that wakes me up sharply. Then the cold, intense cold and more fever – or is it still the first one? I adjust myself in the sofa, yet remain sunken.

A day goes by, two, one week, two months.

And then the fever lifts.

And then my Grandma brings me back to reality.

And I'm hungry.

The laughter of cats

To my sister,
To Michigan and Alanis,
To Emely, Lolo and Lala,
To my Aunt Martha

Cats laugh in a sublime way. They don't burst out in peals of laughter like we do, but in a subtle, harmonious way instead. They do it when they climb on top of us – on our laps, on our chests – or when we pet them, at the feel of our hands on their backs, their bellies, their little heads, and needless to say behind their ears; sometimes they just know that we'll pet them and they start smiling, or when they're sleeping by your side and they reach their paw out to touch you and make sure that you're still there. Yet no one knows exactly how or why they laugh.

I once read that they also laugh when they are dying; I once had a kitten who was killed by dogs, and the last time I saw her, she was laughing, looking at me lovingly and laughing. That's why I understood that the sound their bodies make is laughter, and that they not only laugh with happiness, but also when they need to calm themselves down, like when they're stressed because of many people petting them – in which case it would be nervous laughter – or when they're very hungry. Of course, whenever we feed them, they laugh, and then there they are, laughing calmly as they eat.

There are those who say that that's not laughter, but smiling, but I beg to differ, because their smiles can be seen quite clearly, especially while they're sleeping, and there is no one who can testify that all beings have to laugh the same way. This being the case, cats laugh in the most harmonious way that Nature could have given to any other being on the planet.

Yet most notorious is that cats can be laughing for hours. On this point both science and cat friends agree that the length and serenity of the cat's laughter is to show contentment. How many sleepless nights have I spent when I've been able to prove it, with one kitty laid out over my solar plexus, and the other one curled up next to my hair, both laughing softly until four fifty-nine in the morning.

Yes, the laughter of cats is a singular pleasure.

PART 3

POEM IN THIRTEEN PARTS

The short story of an introverted reality.

I have an agreement of peaceful coexistence with time: he doesn't chase me and I don't hide from him; one day we will meet.

- Mario Lago

Poem in thirteen parts

I

It all ended. I enjoyed it. I went back home. A week went by, five, ten. And now I lament not having enjoyed more.

II

In the most inopportune moment I saw you and I let my guard down. I couldn't bear myself any longer and I gave into your being. Maybe it was the circumstances in which we met, maybe it was that I'd just got back. Maybe it was just your eyes. Maybe it was just my mind.

III

...I'm impatient for you to arrive, because you've got me rather distracted by your absence.
...and now your presence distracts me.

IV

I'm wondering.
Wondering wondering wondering wondering much.

V

And then I turn around and I see you among the trees waving me goodbye in that elegant and abstract way of yours that you've never had, and when I raise my hand to wave you back I realise that I'm still in bed.

VI

And she walked along the peaceful streets. She walked in heels and a jacket. She walked upright, balanced. She walked with a question mark dancing on her clear, white forehead.

VII

I wonder how many times I've woken up. How many times, if we get into it, could I have fallen asleep without even noticing. I often think they could've been twenty or a thousand, or maybe they can't even be counted anymore. The moment you left I woke up again, and someone else came into my life, and then someone else, and I'm sure someone else will come as well.

VIII

During a moment of vigil, an angel arrived.
Incommensurable eyes, sublime lips.
Laughter made of crystal. A jump into the void as I see your eyes watch.

I daydream; clouds, vapours, inconvenient shyness and a little something else.

Impatience gnaws at me; words escape me. My tongue gets twisted at one sole possibility.

Hope frees me and I begin again.

IX

I want to feel your hands all over me,
      as if it was the first time,
      the first time I never had,
that I did have, but I suffered so.

X

My life is a rollercoaster.

Emotions go up and down at the images that go in and out of my mind; passions, longings, wishes that spring up when I least expect them. Songs at the top of my voice that some mistake erroneously for screams. Sorrows that have been left behind and flickers of illusions that run ahead, my faithful guides that ask of me no more than to push forward. Hopes conditioned by my will. Free dreams of dilated pupils. Forced patience in a world in which I don't even remember I live. Tickles in my stomach and in other unmentionable areas, that heal me from an unfamiliar past. Sweetness in his memory, and in his, and in his, and in his…

…but I don't think that in others too. Uncertainty in my future; grace in my confusion.

Isn't it like that for everyone?

XI

I'm surprised by the greatest pain I've ever known, which is also the one that has come least close to make me cry.

I don't know if I'm coming or I'm going, or if maybe everything goes around and around.

XII

An illusory thought woke me up while I was writing yesterday: that fear that I talked about, the shock I caused myself, the distance that I yearned for...

Profound gratitude to you who've come into my way; your presence and your closeness have broken, for once and for all, the pattern that has kept me static for a whole lifetime.

XIII

And the journey begins again.

Graziemille!

With my eternal gratitude to all my beautiful family, who've always given me their support: My parents Soco and Jorge, for their love and trust; my Granny Minerva, my pillar who taught me to be strong since my childhood; my Aunt Martha, my other pillar. My Grandpa Benjamín, whose blood gifted me with ink and letters and who blesses us from the sky; my sister Gina, who's always pushed me in the right direction. My Uncles Robe, Noé, Abraham, Carlos, Manuel, Juan; my Aunts Hilda, Mireya, Paty, Luly, Norma and Alma; men and women from whom I've learned about being noble and resolute. My cousins Cati, Paola, Gely, Noé, Nico, Luis, Chema, Carlos, Toño and Juan, who gave me the most fantastic moments of my childhood alongside Gina, and carry on bringing them on. My brother-in-law Yamil, my cousins Mely, Manu, Carol, Jürgen and Darío, who have bought such amazing things into the family. My nieces and nephews Sara, María and Ian, my cousin Alesa, and the little ones, Jacobo and Galadriel, who have all their future ahead of them and brighten my soul every time I see them. Grandfather Nico, Grandma Noné and Aunt Cuquis, all of who smile down at us from among the clouds.

I also thank my lovely girlfriends in nearness and distance Hillery Keefer, Lulú Rodríguez, Staliana Koskori, Mariana Rodríguez, Rosy Tabares, Valeria Gamboa, Karla Herrera, Julia Joseph and Liz Ruacho; my voice of reason Nikolas Marinakis; the most focussed man I know, Alan Izar; and Sergio Heynes, David Delgado, Konstantinos Michailidis, Spyros Diakakis, Diego García and Erasmo Castro for the long-distnce support; and also Luis G. Galarza, for his permanent smile. You guys have given me the joy of your friendship, plus a healthy dose of light in my soul.

I can't miss out thanking Doctors Martha Palencia and Soledad Ruiz Canaán, as well as Isabel Cisneros, Yemelli Orrante, Kriss Sepúlveda, and Inna Segal and Myriam Quiñonez, for opening the doors to healing for me and leaving me all prepared to head out to the world... Also Mani Navasothy, Vathani Navasothy and Nallely Casillas, who are my friends, teachers and healers all at once, both in nearness and distance... and possibly in every life in which we might've met...

And because the Masters wouldn't have been the same without them, to everyone at Leazes Terrace: Aisha, Michelle, Ibrahim, Christos, Cata, Ana, Monica, Laura, Maria Z, Medha, Aswin, Abishek, Magnus, Andy, Sarah, Manu Bee, Sebastián, Megan, Amit, Duygu G, Duygu M, Meenakshi, Fotis, Maria B, Fredi, Robert, Ann, Mukesh, Neethu, Imran, Duncan, Steve, Andriana, Krishna, Lennart, Natalia, Jamie and Tony!! Thank you for the trips, the laughter, the potlucks, the nice wines and long nights of comradery and support.

And also to those who were not from Leazes but were just as important… Sneha, Cath, Jiihad, Esraa, Lily and Özgür, for the brief but genial encounters, both in class and in any other place.

I also thank three people who came into my life by surprise: Michele Lail, who's taught me that it's not necessary to meet in person for friendship to exist; Erendira Cervantes, who procured me a shining light when I was suddenly in the dark; and Stephen Cole, who is not only teaching me about magic, myths and culture, but has also helped me to translate this book into English, all with love, respect and loads of laughter.

Last, but not least, I thank my wise teachers Ángela Rosas, Anne Aylor, and Jesús Alvarado, for being the initial facilitators of my path; Arturo Kampfner, Olga Santos, Consuelo Mata, Lourdes Niebla y Sergio Quiñones, for believing in me and giving me the chance to exploit all my artistic modalities; Ann Coburn, Will Fiennes, Margaret Wilkinson, Linda Anderson, Tina Garhavi, Jackie Kay, Sean O'Brien and Melanie Birch, for all their support during my MA; Maggie Hamand and Christie Watson for closing London with golden key; and Tina Hartas for giving me my first writing job, hooray!

Note to the 2017 translation: Thank you my darling Khalil – our Little Puck – and sunshiny Max, lovable Julia and precious Fernanda for bringing so much joy and laughter into our lives! And to the Coles, for welcoming me so warmly into their midst! Carol, thanks for all your editing help! And Mike, David, Amber, Elijah and Edana; the Joneses: Rachel, Arfon, Seren, Ryan and Carys; and our amazing Auntie Marion… best in-law family a girl could wish for! … and… to everybody in London and Glastonbury, you know who you are!